Ellie
and
Granny Mac

ELIZABETH
MacLENNAN

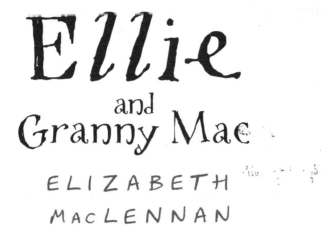

ILLUSTRATED BY

SUE WILLIAMS

For Ella, Scarlett, Eliza, Jamie and Hannah

With thanks to Jenny, Christine and Emma
for their unwavering enthusiasm

E.M.

For Finny

S.W.

First published 2009 by Walker Books Ltd
87 Vauxhall Walk, London SE11 5HJ

2 4 6 8 10 9 7 5 3 1

Text © 2009 Elizabeth MacLennan
Illustrations © 2009 Sue Williams

The right of Elizabeth MacLennan and Sue Williams to be identified as author
and illustrator respectively of this work has been asserted by them in
accordance with the Copyright, Designs and Patents Act 1988

This book has been typeset in Bembo Educational
and Tree Boxelder

Printed and bound in Great Britain by
J F Print Ltd., Sparkford, Somerset

British Library Cataloguing in Publication Data:
a catalogue record for this book is available from the British Library

ISBN: 978-1-4063-1788-6

www.walker.co.uk

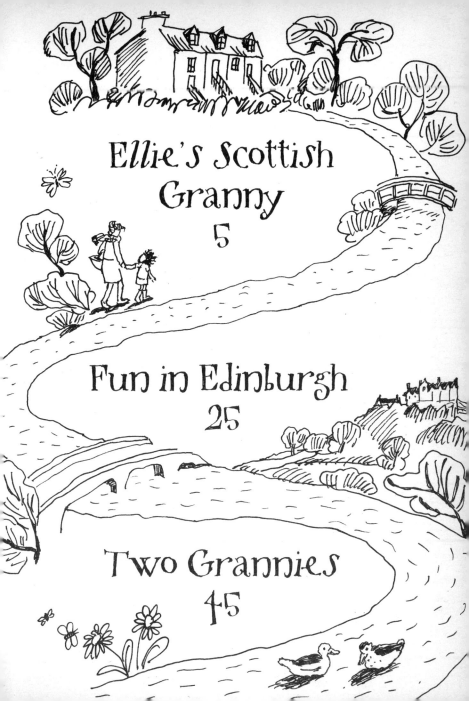

Ellie's Scottish Granny

Ellie was cross. Her Greek
granny, Yiayia, was off to
Australia for the summer.

"Where *is* Australia anyway?"
demanded Ellie.

"Here," Mum said, spinning
the globe and pointing.

"But I *always* stay with Yiayia in Greece," said Ellie. "Every summer. Or else we all go."

"Well, this year things are different," said Mum. "Dad and I are working  away from home and Yiayia is going to Melbourne."

"Why?" asked Ellie. "I need her in Greece."

"You're not her only grandchild," Mum reminded her.

8

"I know that," said Ellie.
"There's Alexi and Irini—"
    "And another baby on the way,"
Mum said firmly. "Yiayia's needed in
Melbourne to help Auntie Voula."

9

"Well, what about me?" Ellie complained, feeling left out. "Who is there for me if you're both working?"

"You can stay in Edinburgh with Granny Mac!" said Mum. "You know you love it when we go at Christmas."

"It's not the same in Edinburgh," said Ellie. "It's *summer* now! I need octopuses and silver fish between my toes!"

"You'll have your wellies," said
Mum. "Granny Mac's delighted you're
coming."

"She makes great chips!" Dad smiled.

"There's the Commonwealth Pool to
swim in," Mum added.

"It's not the sea!" wailed Ellie.

"Or the baths, right near Granny's
house," Mum went on.
"You'll make
new friends
there."

"It always
rains in
Edinburgh,"
said Ellie.

11

"I'll give you a nice hot-water bottle," said Mum. "And you'll have your heffalump. You and Granny Mac can explore the riverbank, and the Botanic Garden. And there's a terrific zoo."

12

"With elephants?" Ellic asked, cheering up slightly.

"Edinburgh Zoo has *everything*," said Mum confidently. "You know Granny Mac makes great scones and raspberry jam. And you can get ice-cream cones and chocolate wafers from the van outside the park gates."

13

"Opposite the swings," asked Ellie, "where we made the snowman, at New Year?"

"Yes, darling." Mum nodded. "He's always there – the ice-cream man, I mean, not the snowman!"

Mmm… thought Ellie. "And then can I go to Greece?" she said.

"No, not till next summer, I'm afraid," said Mum.

"OK," Ellie sighed. "It's a bit of a catastrophe, but I suppose I'll get used to it."

"That's my girl," Mum smiled. "Granny Mac will be thrilled."

On Ellie's first day in Edinburgh, Granny Mac said, "It's raining stair rods!" when she looked outside, and she hurried to bring in the washing from the line.

Ellie laughed. "They say it rains chairs in Greece. Words are funny!"

A fire blazed in Granny Mac's kitchen. They decided to toast marshmallows with a long toasting fork.

"Careful, it's hot!" said Granny Mac.

"I am careful," Ellie said.

"I'll turn it over for you," suggested Granny Mac, and she pulled the sticky sweet off the fork and turned it to toast on the other side.

"Yum," said Ellie, taking a drink of hot Ribena from a mug with "Hibs" written on it. Her wet dungarees were drying by the fire.

"In Greece they'll be dancing in my village tonight," said Ellie sadly, looking at the calendar. "It's the day of Yiayia's festival."

"Never mind, sweetheart," said Granny Mac. "We'll have our own party now! We've got sausages, I'm making chips—"

"Great!" cheered Ellie. "Your chips are the *best*."

"Help yourself," said Granny Mac. "And we can have a wee dance to ourselves while the sausages cook."

She put Aly Bain playing his fiddle on the CD player. It was the bouncy tune that Ellie loved.

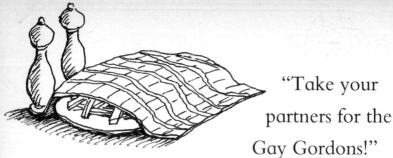

"Take your
partners for the
Gay Gordons!"
announced Granny Mac, piling
the chips on a plate. She covered them
with a clean cloth,
and then they danced
around the kitchen.

"I like that
mushik!" said Ellie,
her mouth
full of
squishy
marshmallows.
"Itsh cheery!"

20

"I'll show you
how to waltz like
your grandpa. He
was a dab hand
at waltzing.
One-two-three,
turn-two-three,
round-you-go-
three!

That's
my girl!"

Then the sausages
were ready.

"Can I have ketchup?" asked Ellie.

"Uh-huh," said Granny Mac. "It's in the door of the fridge. Here you are. Fingers are fine."

Ellie finished everything.

"On Saturday we'll get fish suppers," Granny Mac told her.

"I beg your pardon?" said Ellie.

"Fish 'n' chips and brown sauce. Wrapped in newspaper. Your mum's favourite."

"Cool," said Ellie. "Can I watch CBeebies now?"

"Fair enough," said Granny Mac. "I'll get these dishes done. Then we'll have a story. You can choose."

"I'm enjoying Edinburgh," said Ellie.
"Is it still raining?"

"Like as not," said Granny Mac, "but
we're snug as a bug in a rug."

"Yep," nodded Ellie,
snuggling down
happily on the
sofa with her
heffalump.

Fun in Edinburgh

The swimming pool smelt of bleach. It had wee changing rooms and the door locks were broken.

Before you went in, there was disinfectant for washing your feet.

"My feet are clean," declared Ellie.

"It's just in case," said Granny Mac.

Ellie put on her armbands and swam across the pool. Then she swam back again. She listened to the echoes of children shouting, and thought about mermaids.

A big boy was swimming fast the other way. He bumped into Ellie and water splashed up her nose.

"Never mind," said Granny Mac, "it's time for a shower. Let's wash your hair."

The shower was nice and warm.

"Can I use the hairdryer?" asked Ellie.
They put a coin in the slot and the
hairdryer came on.

Ellie's hair was

very
curly.

Then Ellie put on her red jumper
that Granny Mac had knitted and
they walked all the way up the hill
to Edinburgh Castle. From up there,
you could see all the town below, and
the hills beyond, and the River Forth.
Some soldiers in kilts were marching
past them towards the High Street.
One of them winked at Ellie.

30

Granny Mac said, "Let's get tea
and scones," so they went into a café
and sat by the window and
watched people hurrying past.

The scones were yummy. Almost as good as Granny Mac's. Then it was time to go home on the bus.

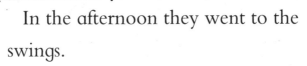

In the afternoon they went to the swings.

Ellie was afraid of the trip-trap bridge. It crossed over the river near Granny Mac's house. There might be a troll underneath it, so you had to run across it *fast*.

Just in case.

Granny Mac said there were no
billy goats Gruff, so the troll must be
long gone. But Ellie was not sure, so
instead she walked with Granny Mac
up the riverbank to the big bridge
where there had *never* been trolls.

There were twin boys in the park
and they looked about Ellie's age.

They had a football, and Ellie
watched them kicking it about.
She liked football, but they didn't
ask her to join in.

After a while the boys went home.
The one called Tom left his jacket
behind. He and Keith had been using it
as a goalpost. Ellie and her granny took
it home with them. It looked new.

"He'll be in trouble," tutted Granny Mac. "We'll bring it when we come back tomorrow and see if we can find them."

Next afternoon there was no sign of
Tom or Keith in the park.

"Let's leave it on the fence,"
suggested Granny Mac.

"Someone could easily nick it,"
said Ellie.

Just then they saw Tom and
Keith coming through the trees.

Tom looked fed up.

Ellie went over. "Here's your jacket," she said, and held it out.

Tom's face lit up. "Great! I was in dead trouble."

Ellie smiled.

Keith said, "Want a game?" and
kicked the ball to her.

Ellie kicked it back, quite far.

They made a goal with some bits
of wood, and Tom put on his jacket.
Then the three of them played while
Granny Mac sat on the bench.

After a bit she got up
and said, "Would you like
an ice-cream, boys? We're
having some."

"Yes, please," they all said,
and together they went to
the van and got 99s. Granny
Mac chose one with chocolate
wafers. They ate them slowly.

"Where do you stay?" asked Tom as they were leaving.

"The Colonies," said Ellie.

"Us too," grinned Tom. "Bell Place. Where are you?"

"Dunrobin Place. Number six."

"See you, then," said Tom.

"Aye," said Keith.

"Uh-huh," said Ellie.

And she and Granny Mac
went home.

"Can we go to the park again
tomorrow?" asked Ellie.

"Why not?" smiled Granny Mac.

Two Grannies

Wherever they happened to be,
Mum and Dad always rang Ellie up
at weekends.

Dad usually said, "Hiya, princess,
how's life?" This time Mum said, "Love
you, shiny moon. Miss you. Big kisses
to Granny."

Granny Mac had a big map of
the world above her fireplace.
Ellie stuck three
silver stars on it.
One on Edinburgh,
where Granny Mac
lived; one on the
Greek Islands, where
Yiayia lived; and one
on London, where
Ellie lived with her
mum and dad.

On Sunday morning, Yiayia rang up from Australia.

"Hello, my little fish," she said, "how's life?"

"OK," said Ellie. "My wellies are on every day. What time is it there?"

"It's supper time here in Australia," said Yiayia. "And I'm feeding baby Irini some broccoli. She looks like her dad and she can say 'Dada Dada'.

Alexi has a tricycle and
he's never off it.
I miss you.
How's
Granny
Mac?"

"She's cooking roast beef," Ellie told her. "We went to the baths. They're a bit smelly, but the castle was brill. I've got some friends."

"That's nice," said Yiayia.

"Boys," added Ellie. "We play football in the park."

"How's the weather?" asked Yiayia.

"Today was sunny!" said Ellie.

"Bravo!" said Yiayia.

"Are you fishing in Australia?" asked Ellie.

"Only once. I caught three fish," said Yiayia.

"Will you pick me up tomorrow?"

"I'm afraid I can't," said Yiayia. "I'll be here for another month."

"You'll miss my birthday," said Ellie. "But thanks for ringing up. Granny Mac says hi."

"I'm sending you a parcel," Yiayia said. "And next summer we'll be together in Greece."

"Promise?" pleaded Ellie.

"Promise. I love you," smiled Yiayia. "We'll talk again soon. Many kisses!"

Granny Mac gave Ellie a big hug
when she came off the phone.

"I'm so pleased you are here," she
said. "When you go away to Greece
I miss you. Let's draw some pictures
and send them to Yiayia,
shall we?"

So Ellie drew the castle

and her wellies

and the ice-cream van.

Then they put the pictures in a big
envelope and wrote on
the front:

Eleni Couvaras
81 Seaview Road
Glendi
Melbourne
Australia

And a smiley face.

Ellie posted it on the way
to the shops.

"Yiayia will be glad to have those," said Granny Mac. "I've still got the pictures you sent *me* from Greece on *my* fridge."

And, sure enough, there they were:

a starfish

and an octopus

and a smiley face,

with love from Ellie.

with love from
Ellie xxxx

"I'm glad I've got two grannies," said Ellie. And she gave Granny Mac a big hug. "Can I come and stay by myself again?"

"Any time," smiled Granny Mac. "Just give me a ring-a-ling. I'll be at the ready!"

"Thanks," said Ellie. "Or you can come to London and sleep in my bottom bunk!"

"Now *there's* an idea," said Granny Mac.